小龍噲噲噲

Lucy Kincaid 著

Eric Kincaid 繪

陳韋倩 譯

三民書局

The Little Dragon   ISBN 1 85854 777 6
Written by Lucy Kincaid and illustrated by Eric Kincaid
First published in 1998
Under the title The Little Dragon
by Brimax Books Limited
4/5 Studlands Park Ind. Estate,
Newmarket, Suffolk, CB8 7AU

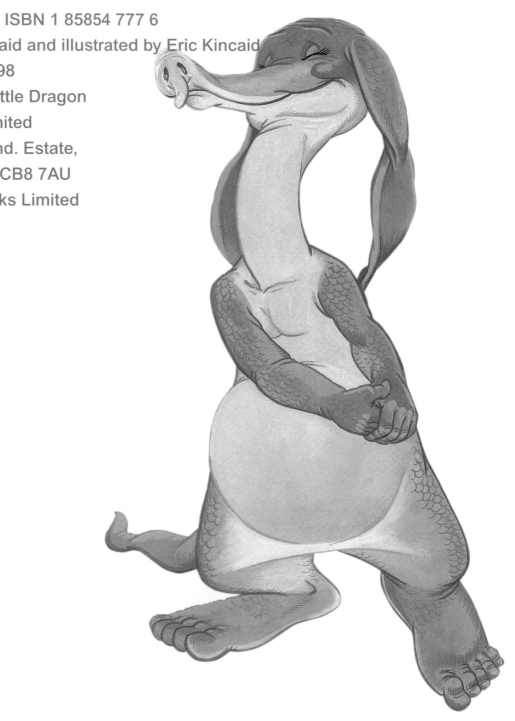

小龍藏身處

Dragon's Hiding Place

One day, Rabbit comes to see Little Dragon.

"What is **wrong**?" asks Little Dragon.

"There are **men** in the wood," says Rabbit.

"What do they want?" ask the bees.

"They want Little Dragon," says Rabbit.

wrong [rɔŋ]
形 不好的

man [mæn]
名 人（單數）

men [mɛn]
名 人（複數）

有一天，兔子跑來找小龍。
「怎麼啦？」小龍問。
「樹林裡有人類啊！」兔子說。
「他們要做什麼呢？」蜜蜂們問。
「他們想要小龍啦！」兔子說。

Little Dragon is **afraid**.
"What can I do?" he says.
"You must hide," says Rabbit.
It is too **late**. The men see Little Dragon. They **run after** him. Rabbit gets under their feet. He **trips** them **up**. The bees **buzz** around the men.
Little Dragon gets away.

afraid [əˋfred]
形 害怕的

late [let]
形 遲的

run after
追趕

trip [trɪp]
動 絆倒

trip...up
使（人）絆倒

buzz [bʌz]
動 嗡嗡叫

小龍好害怕。
「我該怎麼辦呢？」他說
「你得躲起來啊！」兔子說。
可是太遲了。人類看見了小龍，並開始追趕他。於是兔子跳到他們的腳下，把他們絆倒。蜜蜂則圍著人類嗡嗡叫。
小龍逃脫了。

Little Dragon looks for a place to hide. He sees a **hole** in a tree. He gets into the hole.

"What are you doing?" asks **Badger**.

"I am hiding," says Little Dragon.

"I can see you," says Badger.

"What can I do?" asks Little Dragon.

hole [hol]
名洞

badger [`bædʒɚ]
名貛

小龍在尋找躲藏的地方。他看見一個樹洞，便躲進洞裡去。

「你在做什麼呀？」貛先生問。

「我要躲起來呀！」小龍說。

「我看得見你啊！」貛先生說。

「那我該怎麼辦呢？」小龍問。

"**M**en are coming. They want to put me in a **cage**," says Little Dragon.

"I will help you," says Badger.

He **rolls** logs **in front of** the hole.

Nobody can see it now. Nobody can see Little Dragon either.

Badger goes home.

cage [kedʒ]
名 籠子

roll [rol]
動 滾

in front of...
在…前面

「人類快追來了。他們要把我關到籠子裡面。」小龍說。

「我來幫你。」貛先生說。

他把木頭堆滾到樹洞前面。現在沒有人看得見洞口，也沒有人看得見小龍了。

貛先生便回家了。

The men come. They have a **net**. They have **sticks**.

"Where is that dragon?" say the men.

Little Dragon **keeps** still.

The men do not see him. They go away.

net [nɛt]
名 網

stick [stɪk]
名 棍子

keep [kip]
動 保持

人類追了過來。他們拿著網子和棍子。

「那隻龍哪兒去了？」人類說。

小龍一動也不敢動。

人類沒看見小龍，便離開了。

It is **safe**. Little Dragon can come out. But where is he hiding?
Nobody knows.
The animals look for Little Dragon.
Nobody can find him.

safe [sef]
形 安全的

現在安全囉！小龍可以出來了。
可是他躲到哪裡去了呢？
沒有人知道。
動物們尋找著小龍，可是沒有人找得到他。

Little Dragon is still inside the tree. He knows it is safe to come out. He cannot get out. He cannot **move** the logs.

"I will **shout**," says Little Dragon. "The animals will hear me."

小龍還待在樹裡面哪！他知道現在出來很安全的，可是他卻出不來，他沒法兒推開這些大木頭。
「我可以大聲喊叫，」小龍說。「動物們會聽見我的聲音。」

Little Dragon opens his mouth.
But he knows he must not shout.
He is a dragon. Dragons **spit** fire
when they shout. Fire will **burn** the
tree.
"I know what to do," says Little
Dragon.

spit [spɪt]
動 噴

burn [bɝn]
動 燃燒

小龍張開了嘴巴。可是他知道不
可以張口大叫，他是一隻龍哪！
龍一張嘴喊叫，便會噴出火焰的。
火焰會讓這棵樹燒起來。
「我知道該怎麼辦了。」小龍說。

Little Dragon begins to hum. He hums as **loud** as he can.

"Hum hum HUM HUM!"

Little Dragon's friends hear the humming.

"Only Little Dragon can hum like that," say the bees."He must be inside the tree."

loud [laud]
形 大聲

小龍嗡嗡叫了起來。他使勁全力大聲嗡嗡叫。
「嗡嗡嗡嗡！」
小龍的朋友們聽到了嗡嗡嗡的聲音。
「只有小龍才會這樣嗡嗡嗡！」蜜蜂們說。「他一定是在樹裡面！」

The animals try to move the logs,
but they are too **heavy**.
Badger comes along.
"There is nobody in that tree," says
Badger.
"Yes there is," says Rabbit. "Little
Dragon is in the tree. We can hear
him humming."

heavy [ˋhɛvɪ]
形 重的

動物們試著把木頭堆移開，可是
它們實在太重了。
貛先生走了過來。
「這棵樹裡面沒有人啊！」貛先生
說。
「有啊！有啊！」兔子說。「小龍在樹
裡面哪！我們聽得見他嗡嗡叫的
聲音啊！」

"Little Dragon is our friend," say the bees. "It is safe for him to come out now."

"Then I will help you," says Badger. He helps to roll the logs away from the tree. Little Dragon comes out of the tree.

"I'm **glad** to see you all," says Little Dragon.

"We are glad to see you too," say his friends.

glad [glæd]
形 高興的

「小龍是我們的朋友，」蜜蜂們說。
「他現在出來很安全的。」
「那我來幫你們吧！」貛先生說。
他幫忙把木頭堆移開。小龍從樹洞裡走了出來。
「我好高興能見到大家哦！」小龍說。
「我們也很高興能再見到你呀！」他的一夥兒朋友說。

人類文明小百科

一套輕薄短小的百科全書 讓你帶到哪裡就讀到哪裡！

25開／平裝／17冊／100頁

神話
身體與健康
音樂史
奧林匹克運動會
科學簡史
電影
從行星到眾星系
探索與發現
火山與地震
史前人類
樂器
高盧人
希伯來人
希臘人
羅馬人
法老時代的埃及
歐洲的城堡

* 內容新穎而生活化，沒有艱深難懂的文字，更沒有刻板的條列式資料，跟你印象中的百科全書絕對不同！

* 從歷史、藝術到音樂，豐富多樣的主題式探討，讓你學習從全人類的觀點，放眼人類文明，培養開闊的世界觀。

* 豐富的精美彩色圖片，更能加倍激發你的好奇心與求知慾，擴充知識領域與思考深度！

看故事學英文

我愛阿瑟系列

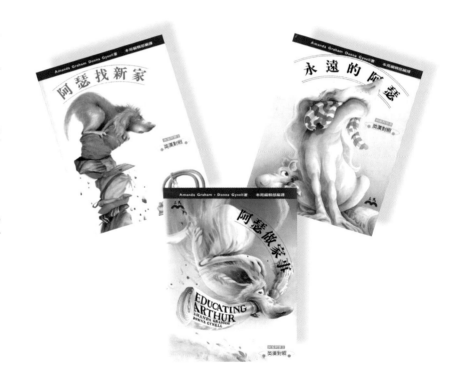

Amanda Graham・Donna Gynell著　本局編輯部編譯

20×27cm／精裝／3冊／30頁

阿瑟是一隻不起眼的小黃狗，為了討主人歡心，他什麼都願意做，但是，天啊！為什麼他就是一天到晚惹麻煩呢！？

一連三集，酷狗阿瑟搏命演出，要你笑得滿地找牙！

他練習游泳、吐氣泡，還有在水中呼吸，
他很努力地練習著，直到他確信，
自己可以當條金魚。
（摘自《阿瑟找新家》）

超級科學家系列
SUPER SCIENTISTS

當彗星掠過哈雷眼前，
當蘋果落在牛頓頭頂，
當電燈泡在愛迪生手中亮起⋯⋯
一個個求知的心靈與真理所碰撞出的火花，
就是《超級科學家系列》！

神祕元素：居禮夫人的故事
電燈的發明：愛迪生的故事
望遠天際：伽利略的故事
光的顏色：牛頓的故事
爆炸性的發現：諾貝爾的故事
蠶寶寶的祕密：巴斯德的故事
宇宙教授：愛因斯坦的故事
命運的彗星：哈雷的故事

網際網路位址　http://www.sanmin.com.tw

Ⓒ 小 龍 藏 身 處

著作人　Lucy Kincaid
繪圖者　Eric Kincaid
譯　者　陳韋倩
發行人　劉振強
著作財
產權人　三民書局股份有限公司
　　　　臺北市復興北路三八六號
發行所　三民書局股份有限公司
　　　　地址／臺北市復興北路三八六號
　　　　電話／二五○○六六○○
　　　　郵撥／○○○九九九八──五號
印刷所　三民書局股份有限公司
門市部　復北店／臺北市復興北路三八六號
　　　　重南店／臺北市重慶南路一段六十一號
初　版　中華民國八十八年十一月
編　號　S85522
定　價　新臺幣壹佰捌拾元整
行政院新聞局登記證局版臺業字第○二○○號

有著作權‧不准侵害

ISBN　957-14-3082-X（精裝）